MW00950900

SCHOOL OF MONSTERS

LEARN
AND PLAY

Fun with NUMBERS!

TEACHER-APPROVED LEARNING WORKBOOK

Sally Rippin

Art by Chris Kennett

Hello, grown-ups!

There are so many ways you can support your child's learning journey from home – the number one thing is to make it fun and relevant to your child's age and stage. Kids learn at different rates and have different strengths. You, the person who knows your child best, are in a great position to support them at the level they are. Lots of learning can be incidental and done through kids observing you and helping you around the house: cooking together, gardening, even tidying can be a fun way of introducing all types of social, physical, and intellectual skills that kids will continue to develop once they get to school.

These activity books have been created by a team of early educators to help introduce your child to some of the concepts they will come across once they start school. Most of the activities are designed to be shared with your child, but some children will be able to attempt some of them on their own. Most importantly, we have worked very hard for every activity to feel fun, but also challenging, which we believe is a great attitude to bring toward a lifelong love of learning.

Now, over to you!

Best wishes,
Sally

The specialist Australian team behind these books are

- **Sally Rippin**, author of the **School of Monsters**
- **Chris Kennett**, illustrator of the **School of Monsters**
- **Ellie Clarke**, Foundation Teacher
- **Gisela Ervin-Ward**, Specialist Literacy Teacher

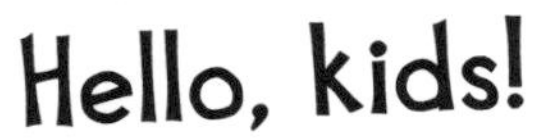

Hello, kids!

Welcome to the School of Monsters! Just like you, these monsters are ready to learn. There are so many games and activities in here for you to share with your helper, and lots of fun things you might like to try on your own. But remember, learning is not a race. We are all good at different things, and we all learn in our own way.

So, turn the page and let these silly, smelly, cheeky monsters share some fun with you!

Lots of love,

Sally

hat

JAM

0 zero

This is the number zero

0 zero

Trace and write the number 0

Find and circle the number 0

1 0 2 4 2
4 0 1 0 3

1
one

This is the number one

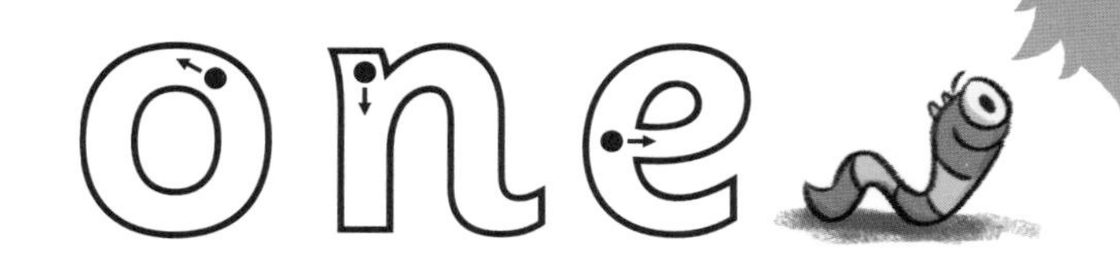

Trace and write the number 1

Mark out 1 square in the frame

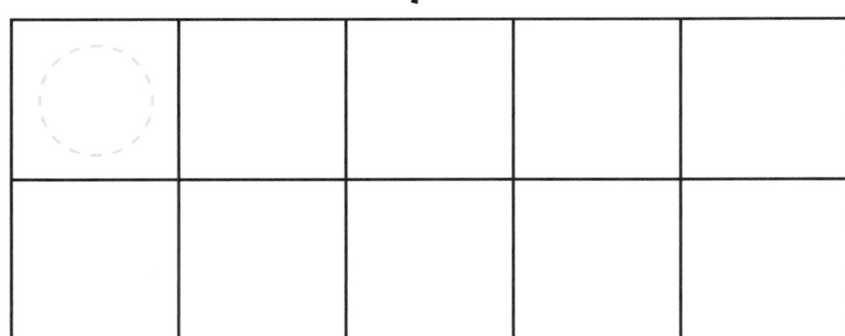

Color 1 picture

Find and circle the number 1

1 3 2 4 2
4 5 1 1 0

2
two

This is the number two

2 two

Trace and write the number 2

2 2 2 2

Mark out 2 squares in the frame

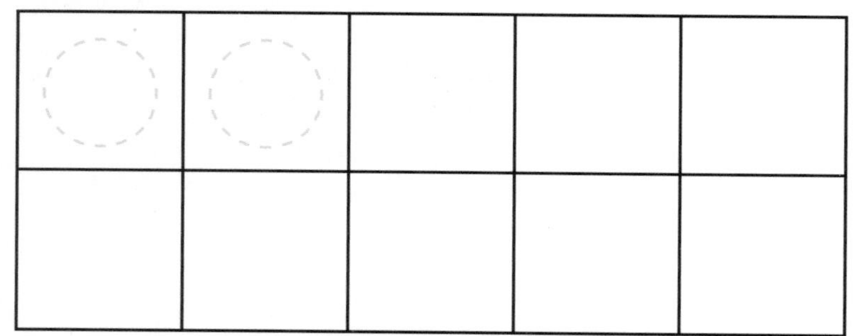

Color 2 pictures

Find and circle the number 2

2 3 2 4 2
4 5 1 1 0

This is the number three

3 three

3
three

Trace and write the number 3

3 3 3 3

Mark out 3 squares in the frame

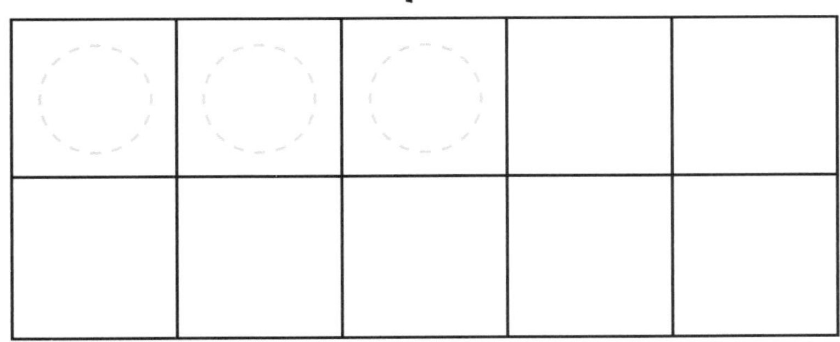

Color 3 pictures

Find and circle the number 3

1 3 2 4 2
3 5 3 1 3

4
four

This is the number four

4 four

Trace and write the number 4

Mark out 4 squares in the frame

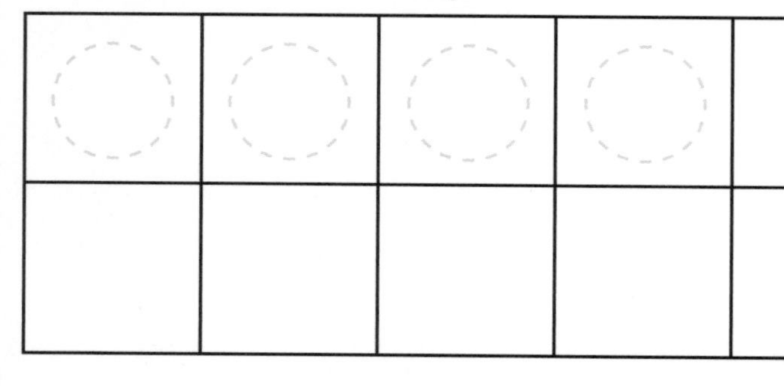

Color 4 pictures

Find and circle the number 4

4 1 3 4 3
2 5 4 4 0

5
five

This is the number five

5 five

Trace and write the number 5

5 5 5 5

Mark out 5 squares in the frame

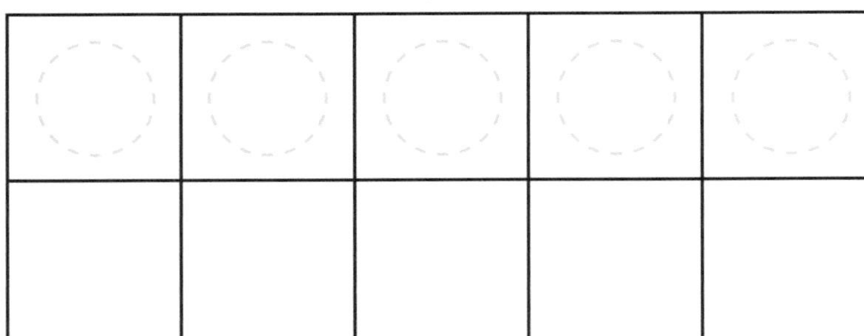

Color 5 pictures

Find and circle the number 5

5 4 5 1 5
1 5 3 2 0

6
six

This is the number six

6 six

Trace and write the number 6

Mark out 6 squares in the frame

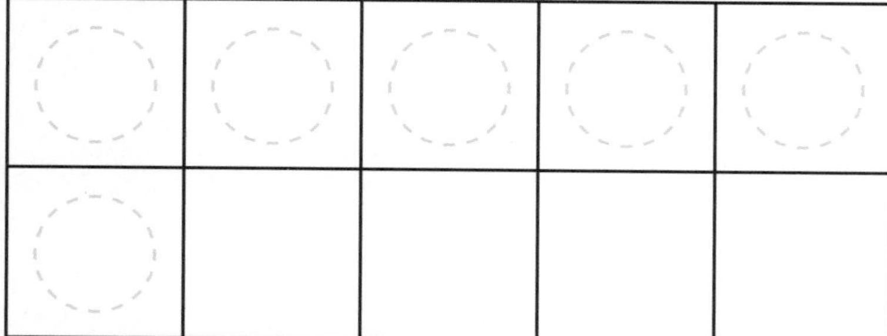

Dot

Color 6 pictures

Find and circle the number 6

6 4 5 4 7
5 7 6 8 6

This is the number seven
7 seven

7
seven

Trace and write the number 7

Mark out 7 squares in the frame

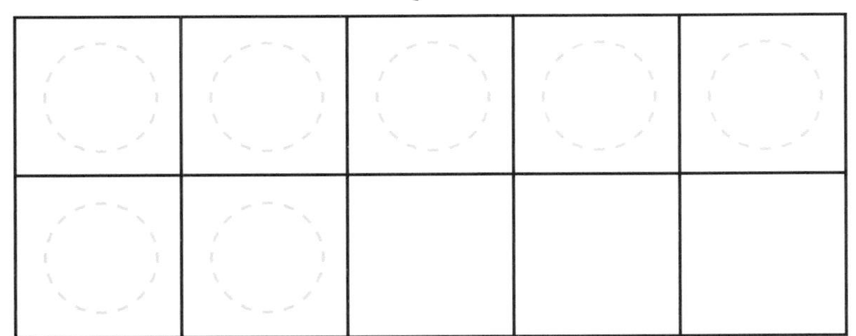

Color 7 pictures

Find and circle the number 7

5 6 7 8 7
9 7 8 7 6

8
eight
This is the number eight
8 eight
Trace and write the number 8
Mark out 8 squares in the frame
Color 8 pictures
Find and circle the number 8
8 7 6 8 8
6 8 9 7 9

This is the number nine

9 nine

9 nine

Trace and write the number 9

Mark out 9 squares in the frame

Color 9 pictures

Find and circle the number 9

7 9 6 7 8

9 8 9 6 9

10
ten

This is the number ten

10 ten

Trace and write the number 10

10 10 10

Mark out 10 squares in the frame

Color 10 pictures

Find and circle the number 10

10 9 11 12
10 11 10 9

11 eleven

This is the number eleven

11 eleven

Trace and write the number 11

Mark out 11 squares in the frames

Color 11 pictures

Find and circle the number 11

11 10 12 11

12 13 11 10

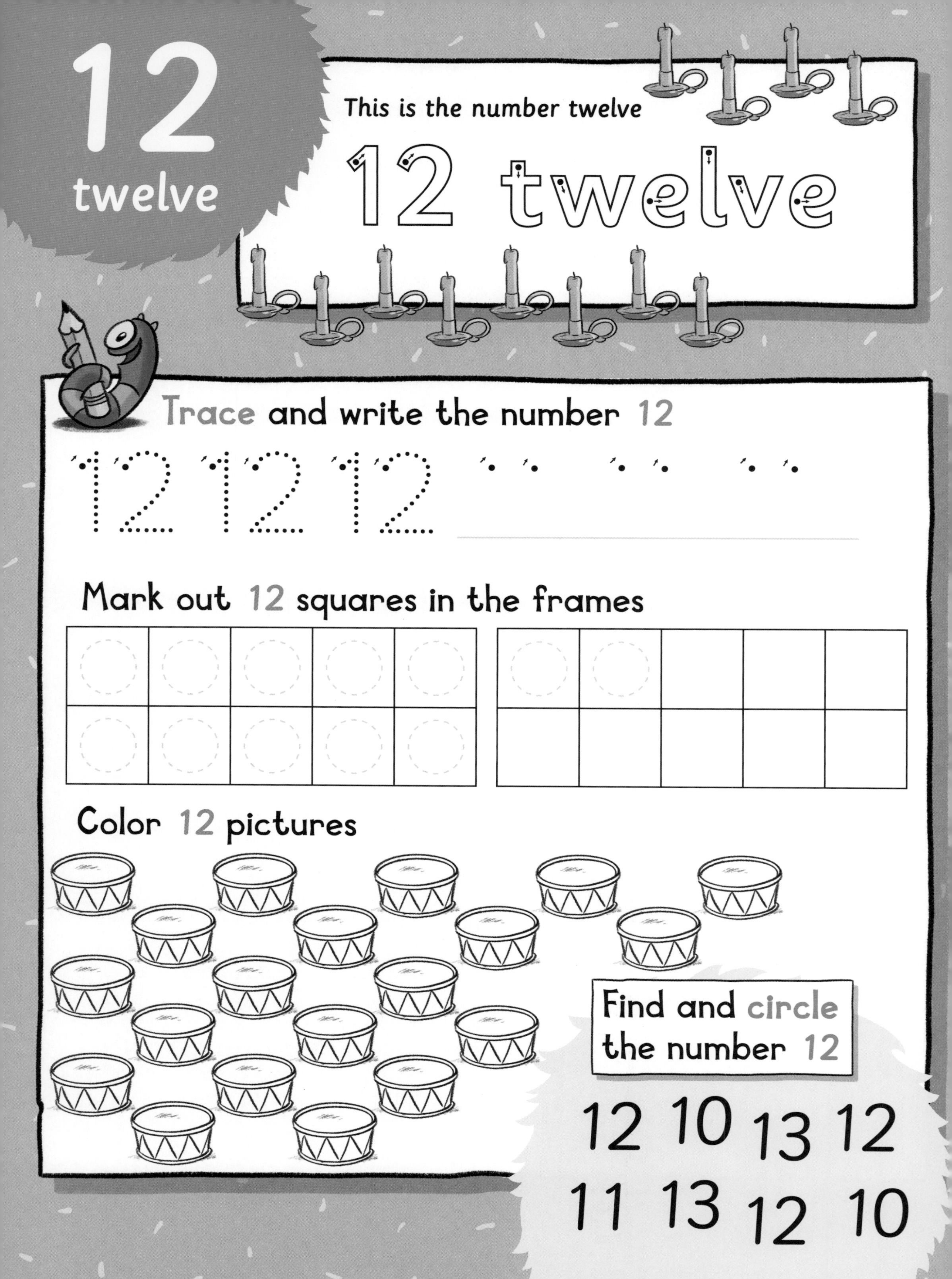
12
twelve
This is the number twelve
12 twelve
Trace and write the number 12
12 12 12
Mark out 12 squares in the frames
Color 12 pictures
Find and circle the number 12
12 10 13 12
11 13 12 10

13 thirteen

This is the number thirteen

13 thirteen

Trace and write the number 13

13 13 13

Mark out 13 squares in the frames

Color 13 pictures

Find and circle the number 13

13 12 11 12

10 13 13 14

14
fourteen
This is the number fourteen
14 fourteen
Trace and write the number 14
14 14 14
Mark out 14 squares in the frames
Color 14 pictures
Find and circle the number 14
12 13 14 12
14 15 16 14

15 fifteen

This is the number fifteen

15 fifteen

Trace and write the number 15

15 15 15

Mark out 15 squares in the frames

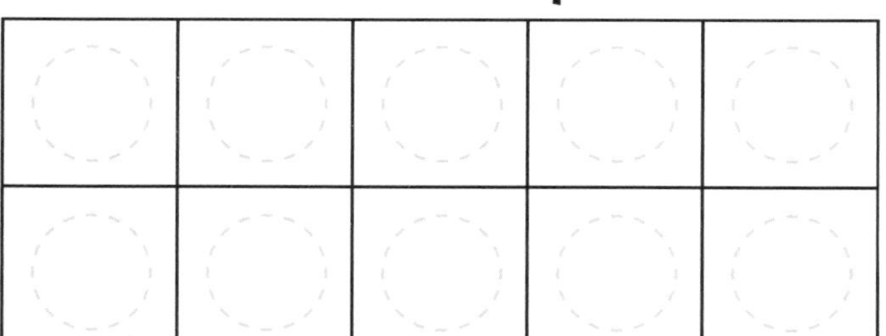

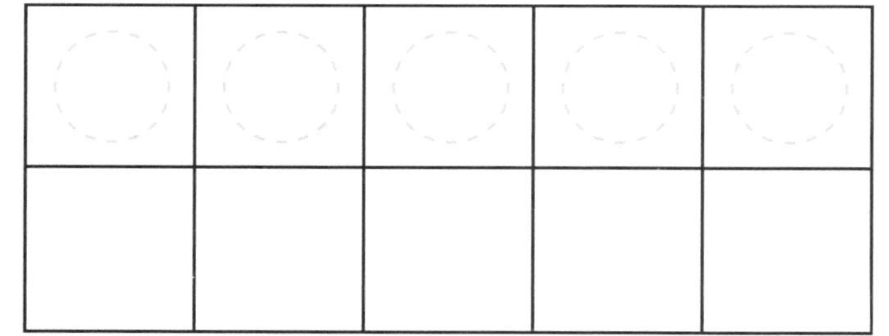

Color 15 pictures

Find and circle the number 15

15 14 16 16

15 13 15 17

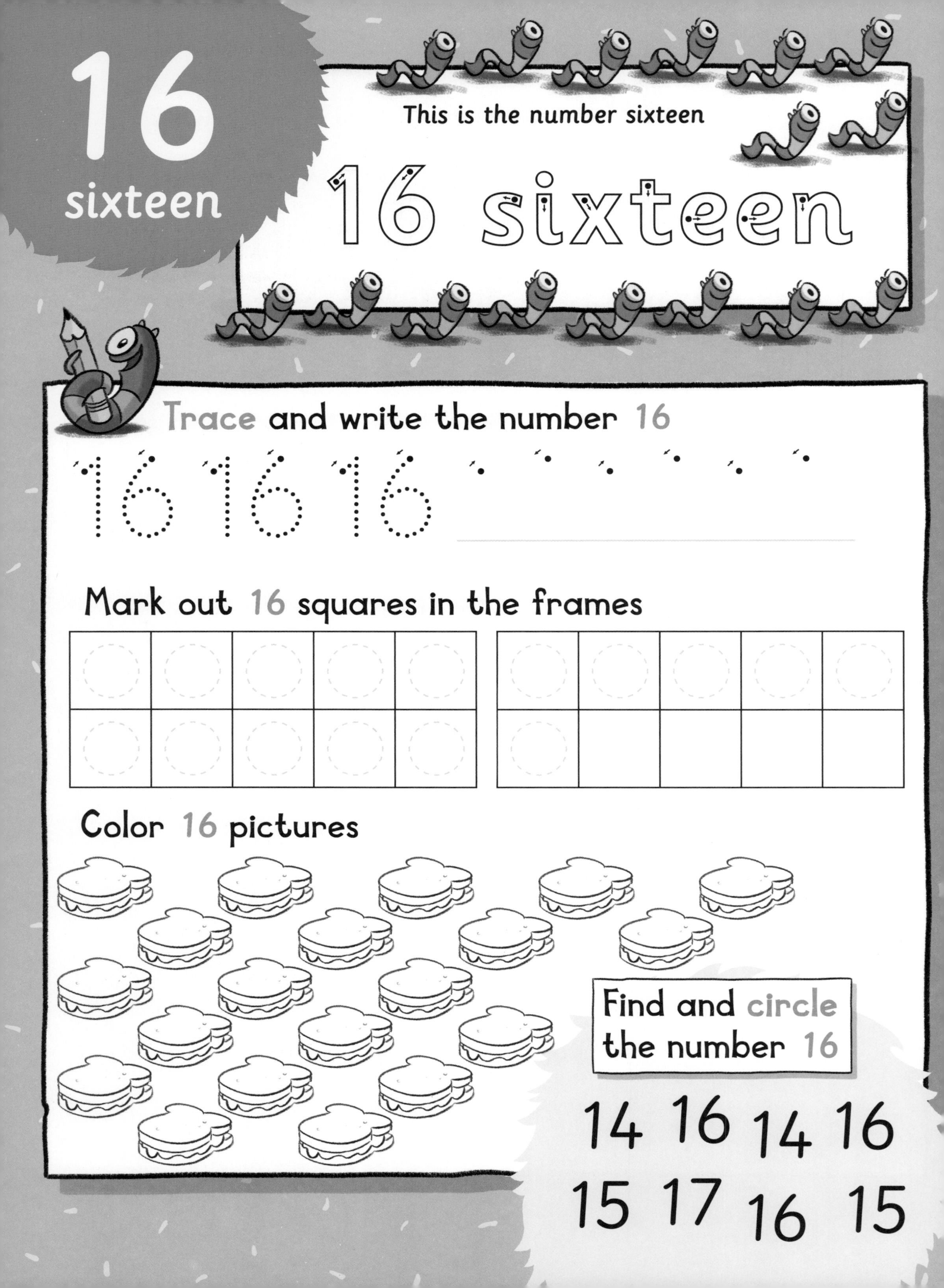
16
sixteen
This is the number sixteen
16 sixteen
Trace and write the number 16
16 16 16
Mark out 16 squares in the frames
Color 16 pictures
Find and circle the number 16
14 16 14 16
15 17 16 15

This is the number seventeen
17 seventeen
17
seventeen
Trace and write the number 17
Mark out 17 squares in the frames
Color 17 pictures
Find and circle the number 17
16 17 18 16
17 15 18 17

18 eighteen

This is the number eighteen

18 eighteen

Trace and write the number 18

18 18 18

Mark out 18 squares in the frames

Color 18 pictures

Find and circle the number 18

16 20 17 18
19 18 18 19

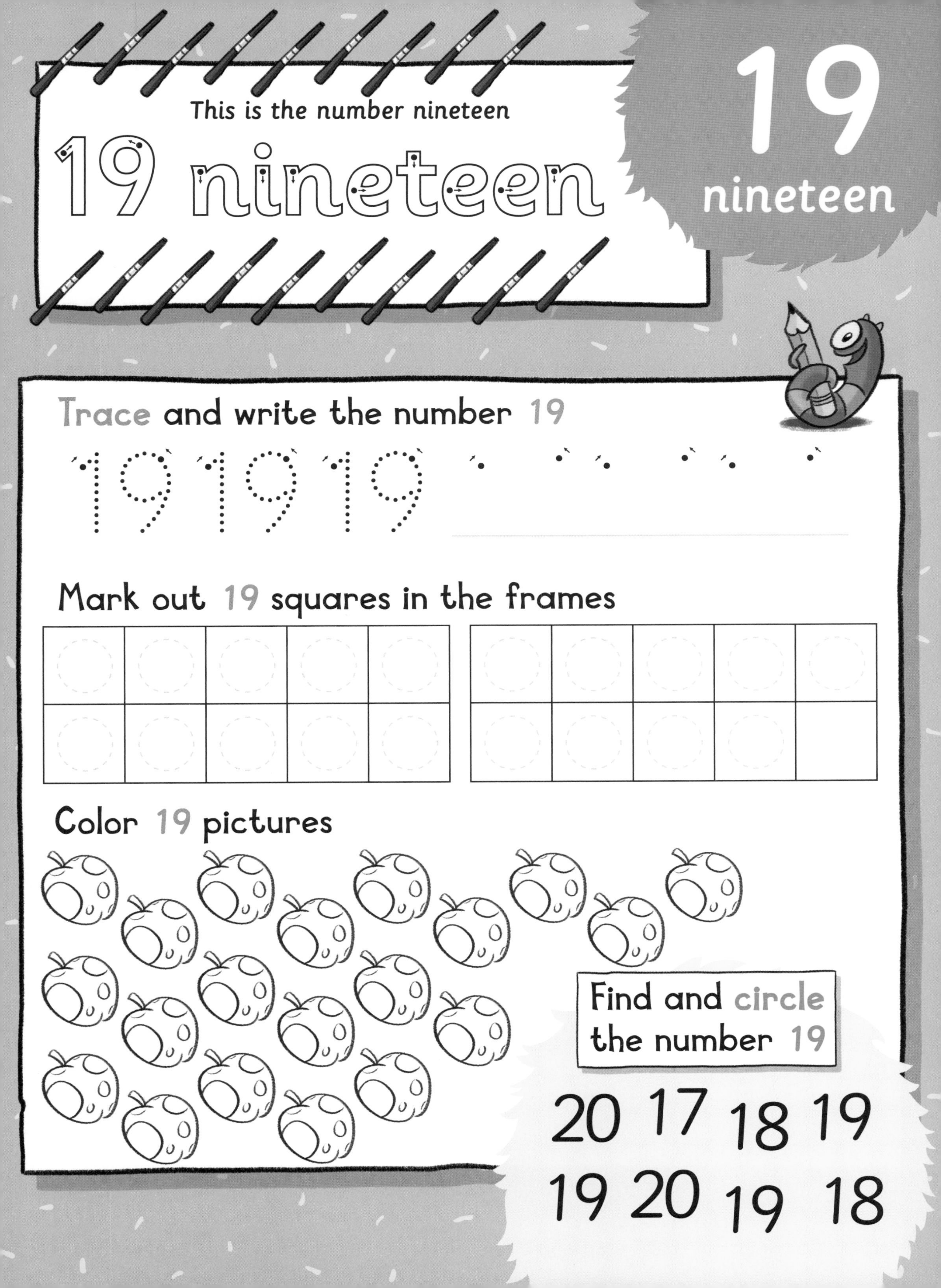
This is the number nineteen
19 nineteen
19
nineteen
Trace and write the number 19
Mark out 19 squares in the frames
Color 19 pictures
Find and circle the number 19
20 17 18 19
19 20 19 18

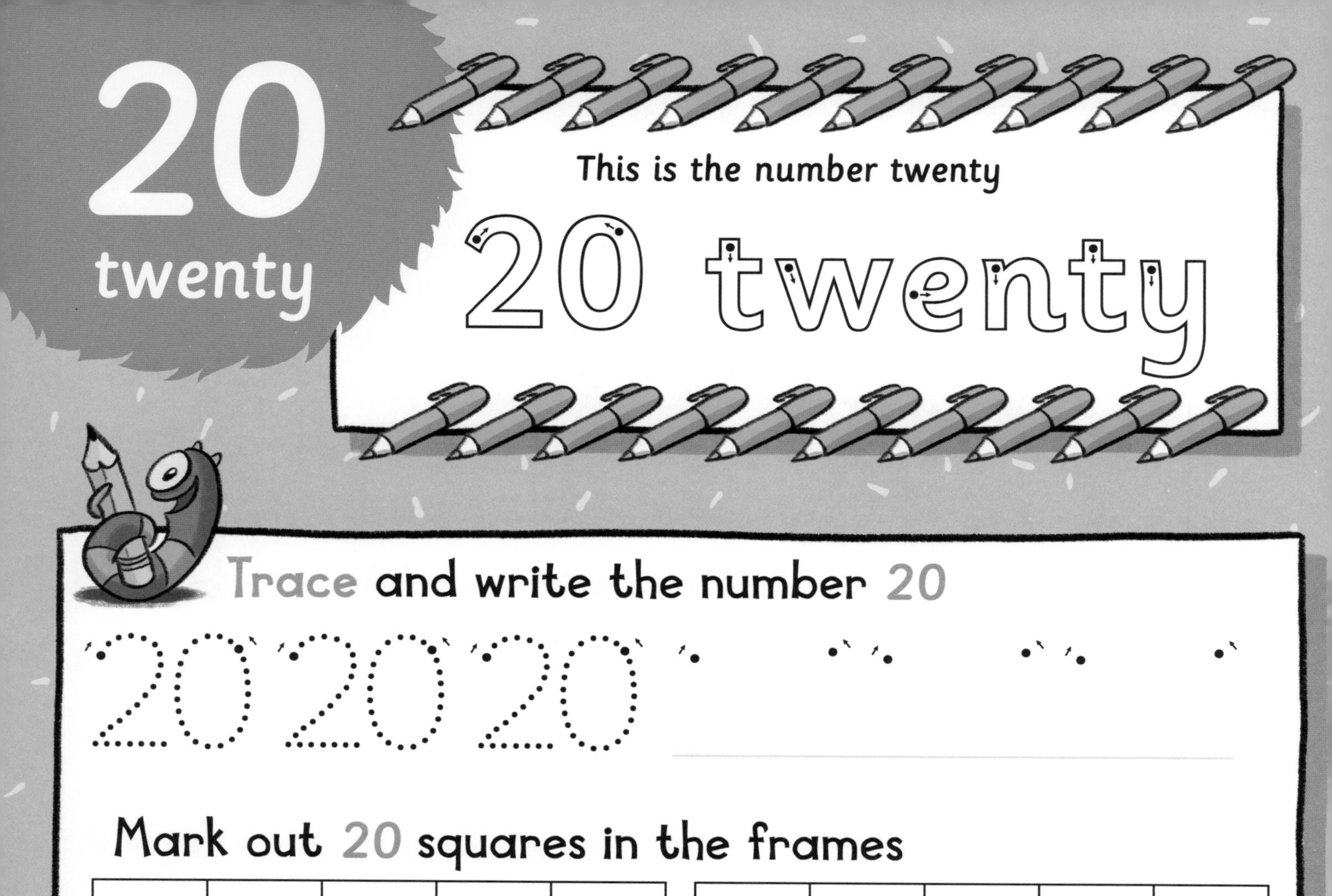
20
twenty
This is the number twenty
20 twenty

Trace and write the number 20

20 20 20

Mark out 20 squares in the frames

Color 20 pictures

Find and circle the number 20

17 20 18 20
18 19 20 19

Trace the numbers

0 1 2 3 4

5 6 7 8 9

10 11 12 13

14 15 16 17

18 19 20

More and less

Look carefully at each group.

Which group has more?

Put a circle around the group that has more.

or

Which group has less?
Put a circle around the group that has less.

or

Write the missing number

Use the number line to help you find the missing number.

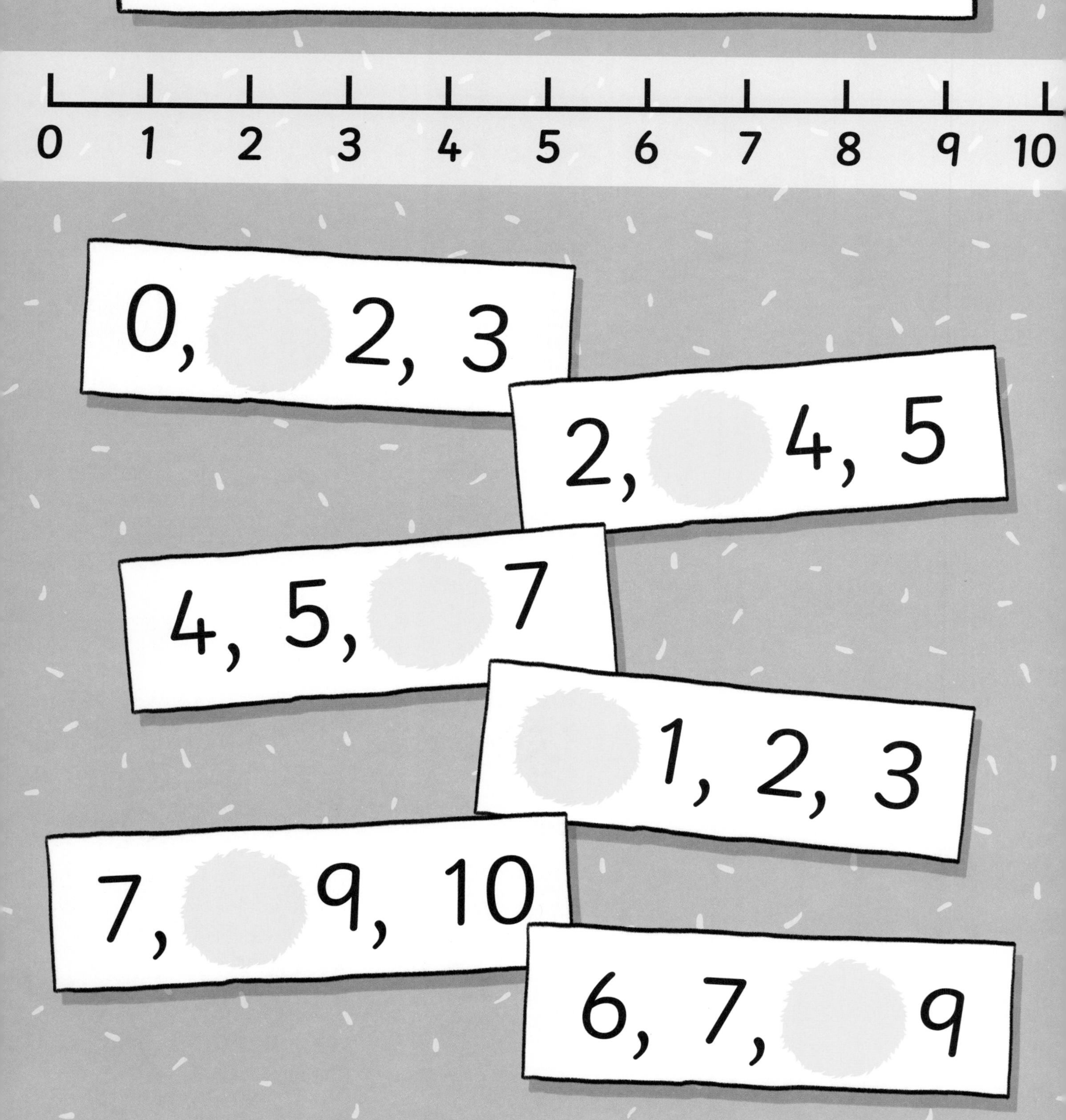

0 1 2 3 4 5 6 7 8 9 10
0, 2, 3
2, 4, 5
4, 5, 7
1, 2, 3
7, 9, 10
6, 7, 9

If you've mastered 0-10, try these...
11 12 13 14 15 16 17 18 19 20
11, 12, 14
17, 18, 20
14, 16, 17
15, 17, 18
10, 11, 13
18, 19,

Match the word and number

Have your helper read each word and then draw a line to match it with the right number.

The first one is done for you.

zero

one

two

three

four

five

six

seven

eight

nine

ten

2

0

1

6

3

4

5

8

10

7

9

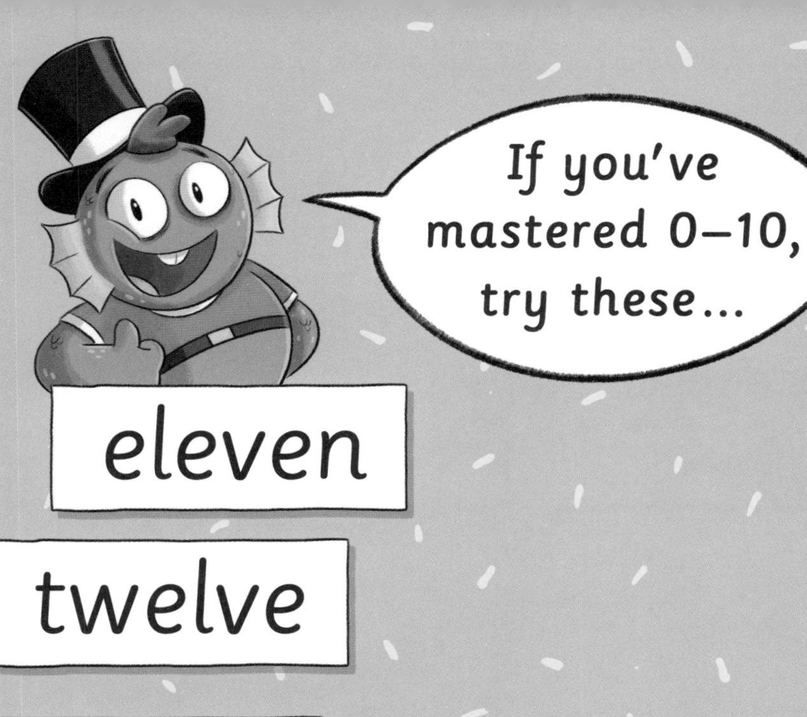
If you've mastered 0–10, try these...

eleven

twelve

thirteen

fourteen

fifteen

sixteen

seventeen

eighteen

nineteen

twenty

13

11

12

16

15

17

14

20

19

18

Dot to dot with 0–10

Connect the dots in order from 0–10 to reveal the School of Monsters picture. Color and decorate the picture when you are finished!

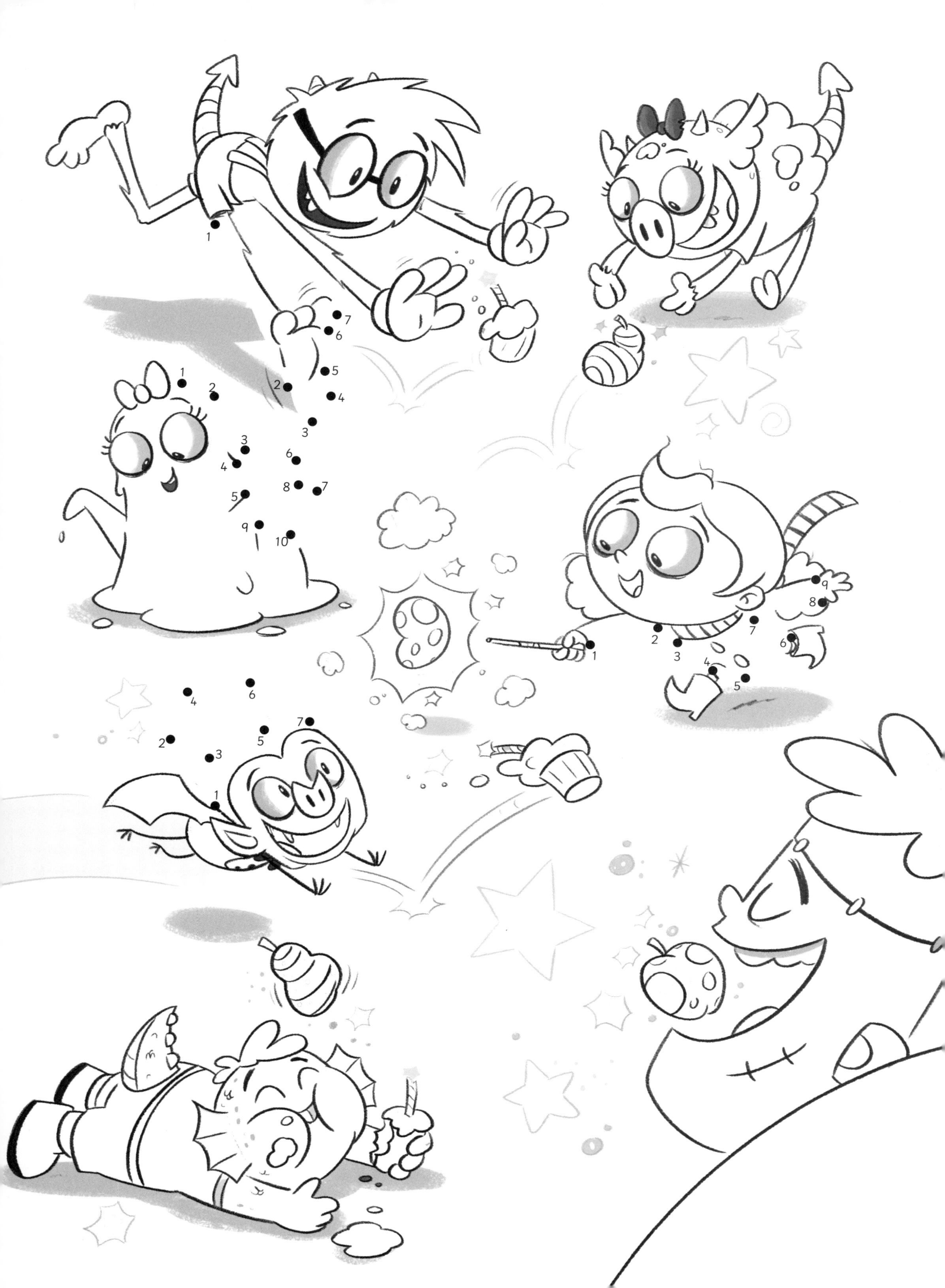

Find the hidden numbers 0–10

Look very closely at this picture.
Can you spot the hidden numbers?
Circle the hidden numbers.

2
5
8
4

7
1
3
6
10

Color by number

Color each section of the picture by matching the color with the number.

Color key

1 Orange

2 Dark blue

3 Pink

4 Red

5 Light blue

6 Brown

Dot

Count and match 0–10

Carefully count the objects in each group. Write the number that shows how many are in that group.

Draw to match the number

Read each number. Draw a collection of items to match each number.

0

1

2

3

4

5

6

7

8

9

10

Dot to dot with 0–20

If you've mastered 0–10 try this dot to dot. Connect the dots in order from 0–20 to reveal the School of Monsters picture. Color and decorate the picture when you are finished!

Find the hidden numbers 0–20

Look very closely at this picture.
Can you spot the hidden numbers?
Circle the hidden numbers.

17
16
15
18
20
5
0
3
8
2
4

13
6
7
10
1
9
19
11
14
12

Finish the number path

Fill in the missing numbers to finish the number path, and meet some friends along the way!

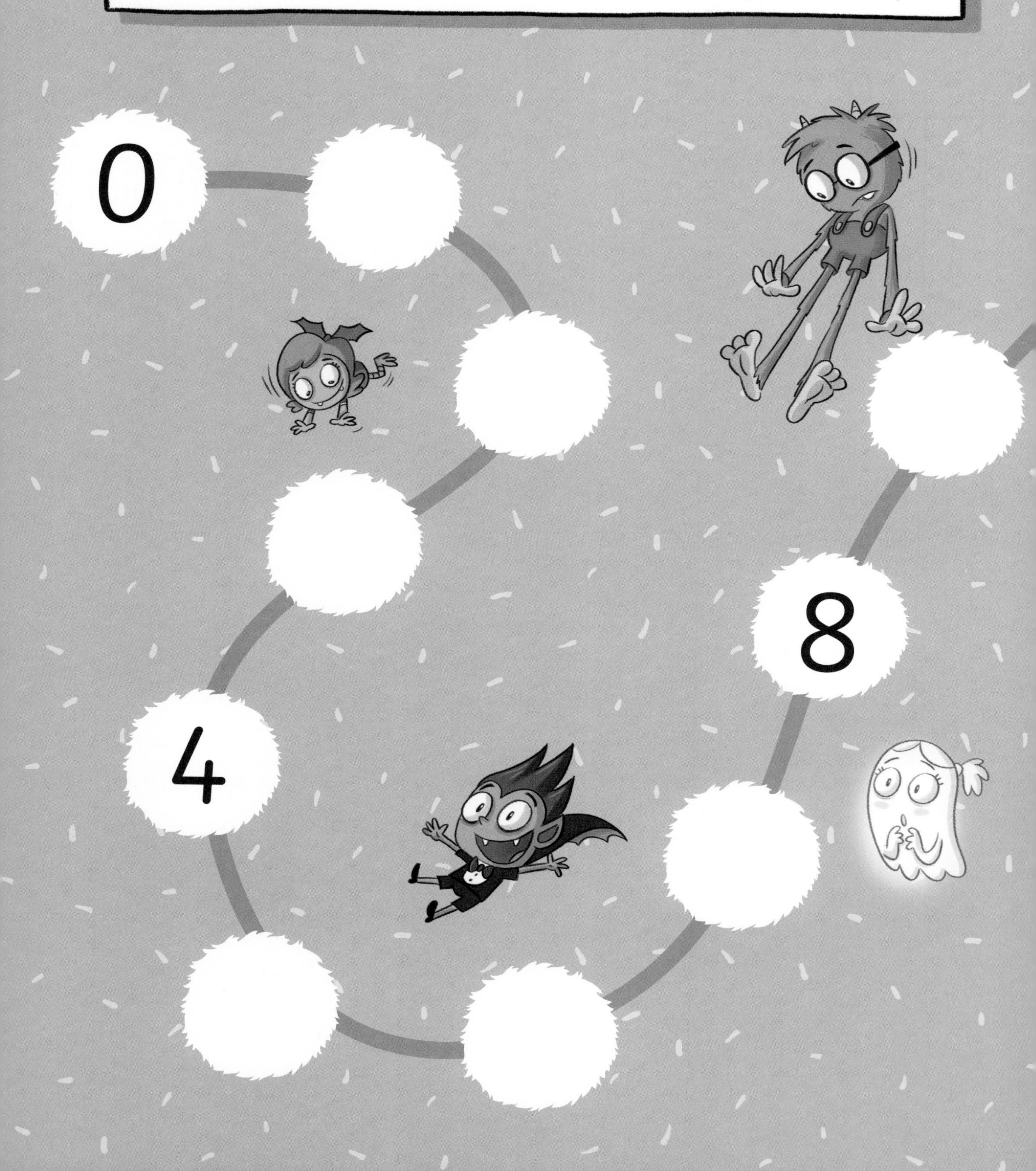
0
4
8

13
16
18

Learn EVEN MORE with the

SCHOOL of MONSTERS

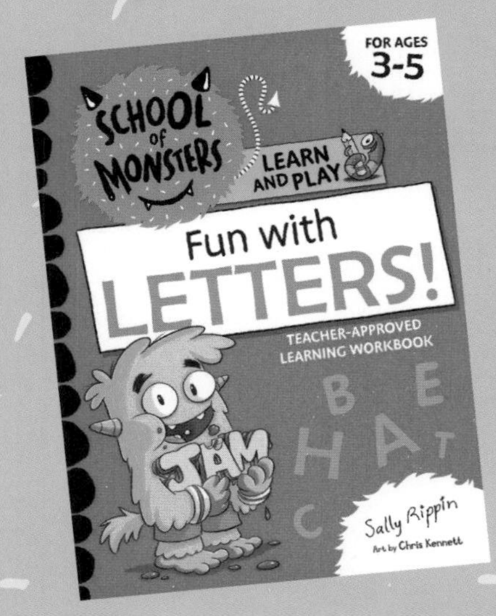
FOR AGES 3-5
SCHOOL of MONSTERS
LEARN AND PLAY
Fun with LETTERS!
TEACHER-APPROVED LEARNING WORKBOOK
JAM
Sally Rippin
Art by Chris Kennett

FOR AGES 3-5
SCHOOL of MONSTERS
LEARN AND PLAY
Fun with SHAPES!
TEACHER-APPROVED LEARNING WORKBOOK
Sally Rippin
Art by Chris Kennett

FOR AGES 3-5
SCHOOL of MONSTERS
LEARN AND PLAY
Fun with WORDS!
TEACHER-APPROVED LEARNING WORKBOOK
BAT
PET
JAM
Sally Rippin
Art by Chris Kennett

Have you read ALL the School of Monsters stories?

SCHOOL of MONSTERS
By Sally Rippin
MARY HAS THE BEST PET
Art by Chris Kennett

SCHOOL of MONSTERS
By Sally Rippin
HAIRY SAM LOVES BREAD AND JAM
Art by Chris Kennett

SCHOOL of MONSTERS
By Sally Rippin
PETE'S BIG FEET
Art by Chris Kennett

SCHOOL of MONSTERS
By Sally Rippin
JAMIE LEE'S BIRTHDAY TREAT
Art by Chris Kennett

SCHOOL of MONSTERS
By Sally Rippin
BAT-BOY TIM SAYS BOO!
Art by Chris Kennett

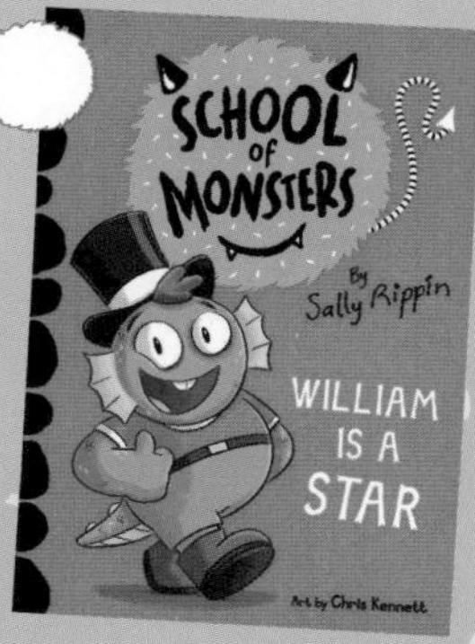
SCHOOL of MONSTERS
By Sally Rippin
WILLIAM IS A STAR
Art by Chris Kennett

SCHOOL of MONSTERS
By Sally Rippin
LUNA BOO HAS FEELINGS TOO
Art by Chris Kennett

SCHOOL of MONSTERS
by Sally Rippin
FRANK IS A BIG HELP
Art by Chris Kennett

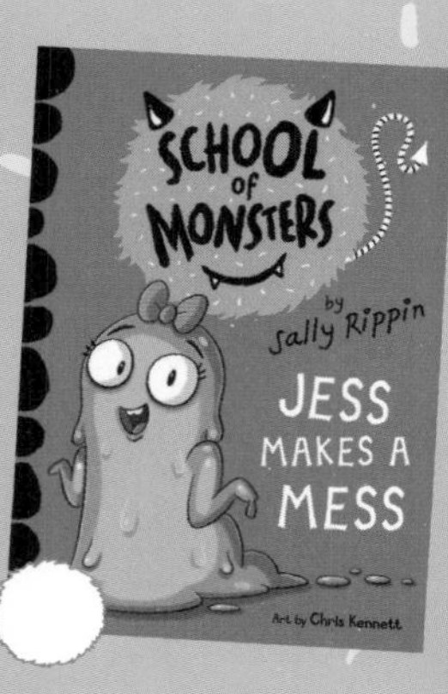
SCHOOL of MONSTERS
by Sally Rippin
JESS MAKES A MESS
Art by Chris Kennett